MEET THE ROBOTS

By Acton Figueroa

HarperKidsEntertainment
An Imprint of HarperCollins*Publishers*

Welcome to Robot City!

Robot City is an amazing place.

It is packed with all types of robots:

big robots, little robots, nice robots,

and some not-so-nice robots.

Meet Rodney Copperbottom.
He is from a little place called
Rivet Town.
Rodney is very smart.
He is also an inventor.
Rodney came to Robot City to meet his hero,
Bigweld.
Rodney brought his Wonderbot with him.
The Wonderbot is Rodney's invention.
It makes him feel safe and reminds him of
home.

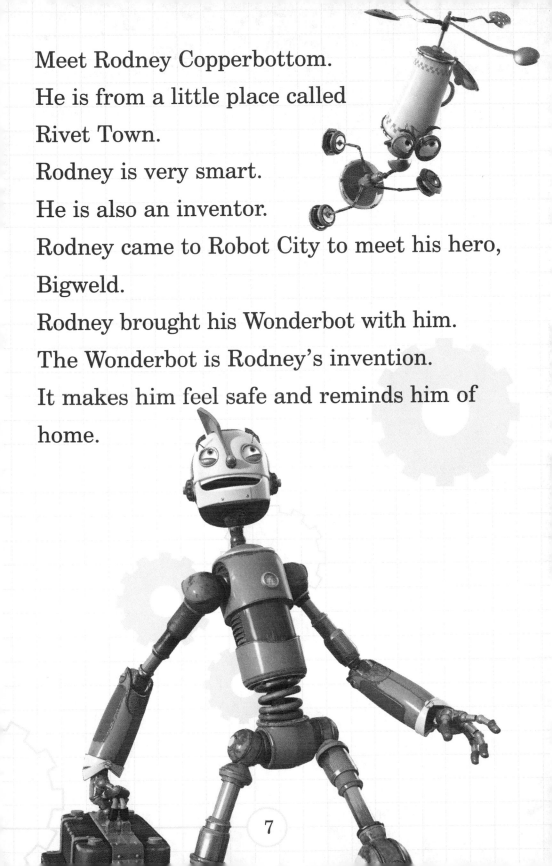

Rodney wants to work for Bigweld.
He only arrived in Robot City a few hours ago.
To Rodney, Robot City is noisy
and a little bit scary.

Being in a new city can be lonely.
Rodney did not know anyone when
he arrived in Robot City.
But he was lucky and made
new friends quickly.

Fender is a funny bot.

He is Rodney's best friend.

Fender is a Rusty.

He is called that because his parts sometimes fall off.

But Rodney is good at fixing things, so he can put Fender back together.

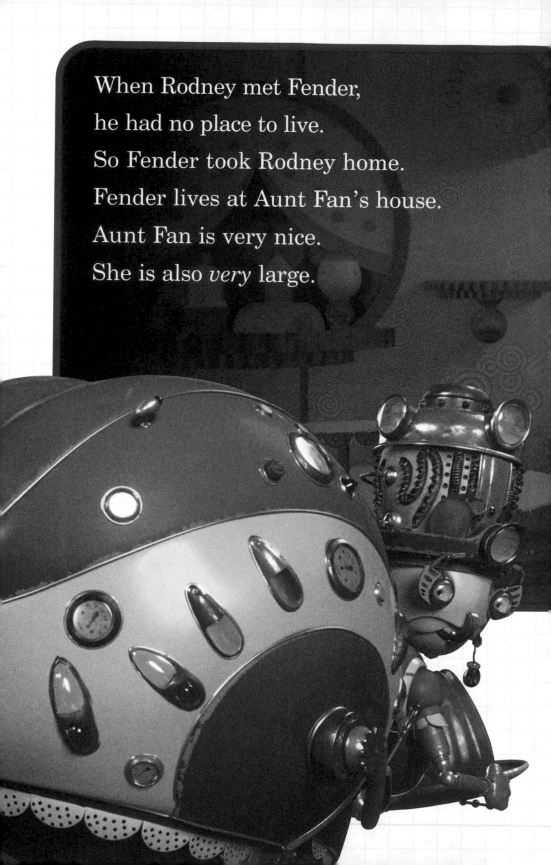

When Rodney met Fender,
he had no place to live.
So Fender took Rodney home.
Fender lives at Aunt Fan's house.
Aunt Fan is very nice.
She is also *very* large.

Aunt Fan takes in broken bots.

(Those are robots who need new parts.)

Fender's friends, the Rusties,

live at Aunt Fan's, too.

Lug is very big, but also very kind.

Crank Casey complains a lot.

Diesel Springer never says a word.

That is because he is missing his voice box.

But he is always on the lookout

for a new one.

Piper Pinwheeler is Fender's sister.

She is as tough as any of the boy robots.

She is also very smart.

Rodney is happy to have so many new friends.
But these are not his only friends in Robot City.

There is one other robot Rodney likes,
and she likes him, too.

Meet Cappy.

Cappy works at Bigweld Industries.

Cappy is from a quiet little town,
just like Rodney.

She moved to Robot City because
she wanted to work for Bigweld,
just like Rodney.

That is not all Rodney and Cappy
have in common.

They both love helping other robots.
And they both look up to Bigweld.

Someone else likes Cappy—Ratchet.

But Cappy does not like him.

Ratchet is not the nicest guy in town.

Ratchet is the boss at Bigweld Industries.
He makes the rules.
The workers at Bigweld Industries are
afraid of Ratchet.

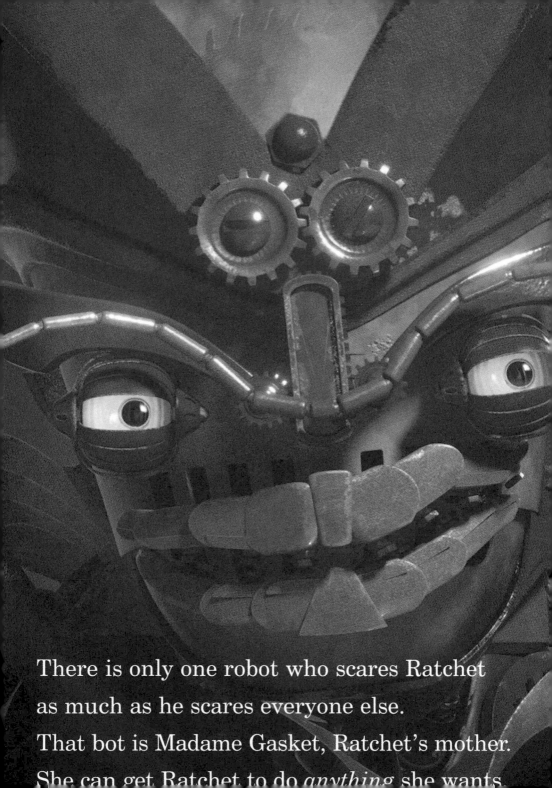

There is only one robot who scares Ratchet
as much as he scares everyone else.
That bot is Madame Gasket, Ratchet's mother.
She can get Ratchet to do *anything* she wants.

Ratchet and Madame Gasket do not
like Rodney.
They want to rid Robot City of bots
with old parts.
They think only new bots are good bots.
Rodney does not agree,
and must stay out of their way.

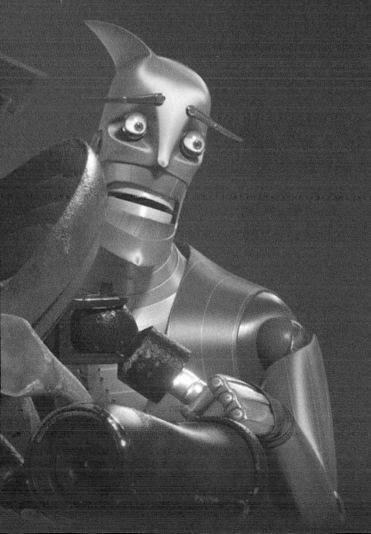

Bigweld does not agree with Ratchet
and Madame Gasket's plan.
Bigweld does not want them to take over
Robot City.

He does not care if a robot is made from
old parts, new parts, or spare parts.
Bigweld says, "You can shine,
no matter what you are made of."

With help from Bigweld, Cappy, Aunt Fan, and the Rusties, Rodney is able to stop Madame Gasket and Ratchet.

Rodney has saved Robot City.

He is a hero!

Rodney and his friends, the Rusties,
are all safe and happy.
Robot City is now a better place,
thanks to Rodney and his friends.